Penny

AND HER DOLL

KEVIN HENKES

GREENWILLOW BOOKS

An Imprint of HarperCollins*Publishers*

Watercolor paints and a black pen were used to prepare the full-color art.

The text type is 17-point Century Schoolbook.

Library of Congress Cataloging-in-Publication Data

Henkes, Kevin.

Penny and her doll / by Kevin Henkes.

p. cm.

"Greenwillow Books."

Summary: Penny instantly loves the doll her grandmother sends her,

but finding the perfect name for her is a challenge.

ISBN 978-0-06-208199-5 (trade bdg.) ISBN 978-0-06-208200-8 (lib bdg.)

[1. Dolls—Fiction. 2. Names, Personal—Fiction.

3. Family life—Fiction. 4. Mice—Fiction.] I. Title.

PZ7.H389Ped 2012 [E]—dc23 2011030043

12 13 14 15 16 SCP 10 9 8 7 6 5 4 3 2 1

First Edition

 GREENWILLOW BOOKS

For Becky McDonald

Chapter 1

Penny and Mama were in the garden.

Mama was weeding.

Penny was smelling the flowers.

"There are a lot of weeds,"
said Mama.

"There are a lot of flowers,"
said Penny.

"The roses are my favorites,"

said Penny.

"I do not have a favorite weed,"

said Mama.

Penny laughed.

Mama kept weeding.
Penny kept smelling
the roses.

"A box for Penny!"

called the mailman.

"Oh, boy!" said Penny.

"The box is from Gram," said Mama.

Penny opened the box.

Mama helped her.

There was a note in the box.

There was something else
in the box.

It was wrapped in pretty paper.

"First let's read the note,"
said Mama.

Mama read the note.

It said:

> Dear Penny,
>
> I saw this doll
>
> when I was shopping.
>
> I thought you would love her.
>
> I hope you will.
>
> > Hugs and kisses,
> >
> > Gram

Penny unwrapped the doll.

The doll had pink cheeks.

The doll had a pink bow.

The doll had a pink dress

with big buttons.

The doll was soft and smelled nice.

Penny hugged her new doll.

"I do!" said Penny.

"I do love her.

I love her already."

"I can tell," said Mama.

Chapter 2

Penny showed her new doll
to the babies.

"Don't touch," said Penny.

Penny showed her new doll to Papa.

"I like her pink cheeks,"
said Papa.

"I like her pink bow.
I like her pink dress
with big buttons."

"I love her already," said Penny.

"I can tell," said Papa.

"What is her name?" he asked.

Penny was quiet for a moment.

"I don't know," she said.

Penny's doll did not have a name.

"Everyone needs a name,"

said Papa.

Penny's name was Penny.

Mama's name was Jane.

Papa's name was John.

The babies' names
were Tilly and Pip.
Everyone had a name
except Penny's doll.

"What if I can't think of a name?"
said Penny.

"You will,"
said Mama.

"You will,"
said Papa.

Penny tried and tried
to think of a name for her doll.

Nothing was right.

Not Polly.

Not Mimi.

Not Emma.

"I can't think of a name
for my doll," said Penny.

"You will," said Mama.

"You will," said Papa.

"Your doll has pink cheeks
and a pink bow
and a pink dress," said Mama.
"You could call her Pinky."
"No," said Penny.

"Your doll has big buttons,"
 said Papa.
"You could call her Buttons."
"No," said Penny.

"Smiley?" said Mama.

"She makes you smile."

"Lovey?" said Papa.

"You love her already."

"There's always Dolly," said Mama.

No. No. No.

Nothing was right.

Penny hugged her doll.

"Don't worry," she said.

"I will find a name for you."

Chapter 3

Penny still could not think
of a name for her doll.
"Try not to think too hard,"
said Mama.
"Then maybe a name
will come to you," said Papa.
"Okay," said Penny.
"I will show my new doll
her new home."

Penny showed the kitchen
to her doll.

"This is where we cook,"
said Penny.

Penny showed her bedroom
to her doll.

"This is where we sleep,"
said Penny.

Penny showed the bathroom
to her doll.

"This is where we take a bath,"
said Penny.
"But you can't get wet."

Then Penny took her doll
to the garden.

"This is where I was
when I got you," she said.

Penny let her doll

smell the roses.

Penny was quiet for a moment.

Then she ran into the house.

Penny found Mama and Papa.

"I know her name!" she said.

"What is it?" asked Mama.

"What is it?" asked Papa.

Penny held up her new doll.

"Mama, Papa," she said,

"this is Rose!"

"Beautiful," said Mama.

"Wonderful," said Papa.

The babies made baby noises.

Penny smiled.

"You said a name

would come to me,

and it did."

Penny hugged Rose.

"Now you can stop
thinking so hard," said Mama.

"Now we can eat lunch," said Papa.

"And now everyone has a name,"
said Penny.